Biff, Anneena and Nadim were
watching a film about bush fires
in Australia.

1

"What happens to the animals when there are fires?" asked Nadim.
"I don't know," said Biff.

The magic key began to glow.
It was time for an adventure.

The magic key took them to a beach.
"Oh no! Look at all that smoke,"
said Biff.

A boy ran out of the sea.
"Nan!" he yelled. "There's a bush fire!
We should go."

"Quick, Ben!" shouted Nan. "We must run home! I'll call the fire service."
"Can we help?" asked Anneena.

Ben said that they must run back
to his house. "You can help us spray
water on the roof and walls."

"It's hard for koalas when there are bush fires," panted Ben. "Birds can fly away, but not the koalas."

"The helicopter will come soon to drop water," said Nan. "But we can't wait! Quick! Get the hoses going."

Biff and Anneena found a hose.
Nadim turned it on. They aimed
the water at the walls.

"Ben, run and tell old Mrs Wilson to come outside with us," said Nan.
"We must all get ready to leave."

Ben and Nadim shouted and banged at Mrs Wilson's door, but she didn't come and open it.

They raced to the back of the house.
They ran inside but they still couldn't
find Mrs Wilson.

Just then, they saw the old lady.
"I was looking for Bunyip," she said.

"Where's the helicopter?" said Biff.
"I can hear it!" said Anneena.

Just then the helicopter flew over.
It began to dump water on the
trees nearby.

"How does that help?" asked Nadim.
"If the trees are really wet, the fire
won't spread this way," said Ben.

Another helicopter flew over.
It dumped water on the trees behind
the houses.

The pilot waved to the children.
"It will come back with more water,"
said Nan. "But we must leave soon."

"A koala with a joey" said Anneena.
"They'll be hot," said Nan. "And they
might be thirsty."

"Do they drink water?" asked Biff.
"Let's see," said Nan.
She filled Bunyip's bowl with water.

"The helicopters have stopped the fire for now, but we must be on our way," said Nan. "Thank you for helping."

"It's good we could help," said Biff.
"And we've seen koalas!" said Nadim.
The magic key began to glow.

"What a scary adventure!" said Biff.
"But at least we helped the koalas,"
said Anneena.